No Problem!

by Jan Weeks

illustrated by Terry Denton

Characters

Jack, that's me

Mum

Contents

Chapter 1

Orders from Mum

It was Sunday afternoon. I was in my bedroom watching a good movie about aliens when Mum poked her head in. You could tell by the look on her face that she wasn't happy.

"Just look at the state of this room, Jack," she said. "It looks like a pigsty. Turn off the television and clean it up."

"In a minute," I answered, wishing she'd go away. The aliens were about to attack Earth and I wanted to see what was going to happen.

Mum was always trying to wreck my fun. What if my room was a mess? It didn't bother me. I liked it that way. It was a waste of time making my bed when I was only going to sleep in it again. Hanging up clothes was just as stupid. I could always find what I wanted to wear on the floor.

"Now!" Mum insisted, in her you'd-better-hurry-up-and-do-it voice. "This is the last time I'm going to ask you, Jack. Tidy your room or you're going to be sorry."

"Do this! Do that! She never leaves me alone!" I thought. When the movie finished, I watched cartoons. After that, there was car racing. That was more fun than tidying my dumb room.

Chapter 2

On My Own

It was time for dinner. Mum had made pizza. I could smell it. "Yum!" I said as I dashed into the kitchen. Pizza is my favourite food.

Mum and Dad were already sitting at the table. Not only that! They'd almost eaten the whole pizza.

"How come you didn't call me?" I asked. It wasn't like them to be so greedy.

"It could be because you're not having any," Mum answered.

It was then that I saw that the table was only set for two people. "Why not?" I asked, wondering what was going on.

"If you're not going to tidy your room, Jack, I'm not doing anything for you. That includes cooking your meals," said Mum.

"What am I supposed to eat?" I asked.

"Whatever you make for yourself," Mum answered. "There's plenty of food in the house."

"This is taking things a bit far," I thought. "It's a mother's job to look after her kid."

I looked at Dad, expecting him to stick up for me. He just said, "Your mother isn't your slave."

"OK," I said. "No problem! Do nothing for me. I'll be fine on my own!"

"We'll see," Mum said. "If you do tidy your room, I might change my mind."

No way! I liked my room exactly the way it was. Messy!

For dinner I had a bowl of cornflakes.

Chapter 3

Not My Fault

When I woke the next morning, it was quiet. I thought it must be early. Then I saw the time.

Mum should have woken me! It was a quarter to nine. That meant I had fifteen minutes to dress, have breakfast and get to school.

My teacher doesn't like kids being late — especially when you don't have a good excuse. I rushed into the kitchen. Mum was reading the newspaper.

"I don't have time for breakfast," I told her. "I'm going to be late for school."

"You're going to have to learn to get up earlier," Mum answered.

I asked Mum where she'd put my lunch. Usually it was on the bench.

"Oh, I don't do lunches," Mum said. "You have to make your own sandwiches."

"I'm already late," I grumbled. "You're going to have to drive me to school."

Mum shook her head. "I don't think so, dear. I don't run a taxi service. You'll have to walk."

Grabbing my school bag, I raced out the door. Thanks to Mum, I didn't have a hope of getting to school on time.

On the way I tried to think of a good excuse to tell my teacher. I decided it was easier to tell Mr Jones the truth.

School had already gone in. Everybody looked at me as I walked into the classroom. "It's not my fault I'm late," I mumbled. "Mum didn't wake me."

"I bet if you were going to Wonderland or the beach you wouldn't need your mother to wake you," Mr Jones said.

"You can stay in at lunchtime to catch up on the work you've missed."

I didn't have anything to eat at recess. By lunchtime I was starving. I wrote myself a note to make peanut butter sandwiches for lunch tomorrow.

Chapter 4

Cornflakes Again!

I play trumpet in the school band. After school on Monday we always have band practice.

When we started playing the sky looked a bit black. By four o'clock it was pouring. "No worries," I said to myself. "Good old Mum will pick me up in her car."

Only there was no sign of Mum. I had to walk home in the rain. By the time I got there I looked like a drowned rat. Mum was sitting in a chair on the front porch having a cup of tea.

"Did you get a little bit wet, dear?" she asked.

"Don't talk to me," I answered.

I went into the kitchen to get myself something to eat. The dirty plate and spoon I'd used the night before were still sitting on the sink. Beside them was a sign that said 'Jack's Things'. I'd also been given a dinner plate, a mug, a knife and a fork.

"I don't do washing up either," Mum said, following me. "You use them, you wash them."

The clothes that I'd worn over the weekend had been picked up from the bathroom floor and thrown onto my bed. So had all the other things I'd left lying around the house, like my cricket bat, my bike helmet and my soccer boots. It made my room look messier than ever.

I didn't care. I just pushed the whole lot onto the floor. It was Mum's silly game. We'd see who grew tired of it first. It wasn't going to be me.

That night my parents had Chinese take-away for dinner. I had another bowl of cornflakes.

Chapter 5

Nothing to Wear

It rained all week. By Thursday afternoon all my school clothes were in a soggy pile in the corner of my bedroom. They were beginning to smell.

I had nothing left to wear. I decided to do some washing. How hard could it be?

I dumped my clothes into the washing machine. I didn't know how much soap was needed, so I used it all. So what if the box was nearly full! Mum would just have to buy some more.

I went into my bedroom to watch TV. The room didn't look half as messy without all those smelly, wet clothes.

Later, I heard a scream. It came from the laundry. I went to have a look. Mum was up to her ankles in pink soap suds. They were bubbling out of the washing machine, down its sides and over the floor.

"Whoops!" I said. "I must have used too much soap."

"How much did you use?" Mum asked as she grabbed the mop.

"All of it," I answered.

Then she wanted to know why the bubbles were pink. It turned out that my new red T-shirt had run. It made everything else in the machine pink. I didn't know that would happen. I hoped the pink would come out of all my white shirts.

"And you still think you can take care of yourself," Mum said, shaking her head.

I didn't anymore. It was all too hard. I wanted things back to the way they were before. I needed someone to take care of me. I was still a kid. I wasn't ready to do grown-up things.

It was time to give in. "I think I might tidy my room now," I said. And Mum thought it was the best idea she'd heard all week.

Glossary

dumped
thrown down without looking

excuse
reason why something happened

greedy
to eat more than you need

pigsty
a pen where pigs live; a messy place

pizza
a flat bread covered by cheese, tomato and other toppings

recess

playlunch, break
during the morning

slave

a person who is
made to work very
hard for someone else

soggy

wet and heavy

suds

soapy foam

Jan Weeks

Can you answer these questions about Jack using only letters?

1. What does Jack say when he means yes?
2. Jack's bucket is this when it has nothing in it.
3. This is Jack's favourite animal. It lives in the water and can balance a ball on its nose.
4. Holes in Jack's teeth are caused by this.
5. Jack finds making a mess opposite to hard.
6. This is something Jack says when he sees a pretty girl.

Answers
1. OK 2. MT 3. CL 4. DK 5. EC 6. ICAQT

Terry Denton